Aloha Christmas

BURTON RICHARDSON

To contact the author for media engagements or for signed copies, email:
info@burtonrichardson.com

Thanks to Artist Mae Waite for her illustrations.
And thanks to Editor Brandon Bosworth and to Layout Artist Deborah Perdue.

ISBN: 979-8-9872462-0-7

Interior design and cover design:
Deborah Perdue: www.illuminationgraphics.com

Dedication

To my wonderful wife Sarah. I love that you love books, especially this one.

To our amazing daughter Talina
for being an exemplary Ambassador of Aloha.

To each of you around the world who spread Aloha by living Aloha.

CHAPTER ONE

The warm sand and shimmering turquoise ocean of Waikiki welcomed both tourists and locals alike, embracing them as a parent would a child in need of loving reassurance. Everyone was all smiles, soaking in the caress of the sea and the warmth of the sun, especially those who had voyaged from snowy climes for a brief respite in paradise.

Tourists waited in line to take a photo with the statue of Duke Kahanamoku. Someone had placed a Santa hat on the famous surfer's head, and everyone wanted to send a picture from the islands to their friends, rubbing in the fact that they were cruising in board shorts while those back home were scraping ice off their windshields. In beloved Hawaii, the only way to tell that the holiday season had arrived was by all the Christmas décor.

While tourists and locals alike relaxed, Pono Kalele lugged his large, 34-year-old Polynesian frame into the back of the delivery truck parked beside the outdoor stage near Duke's statue. He disappeared into the shade and rustled around. His co-worker Makoa was curious. "Pono, wat' you doing brah?"

More rustling. Makoa playfully knocked on the metal door. "I waiting."

"Keep yo' slippahs on", replied Pono.

Makoa looked down at his worn Surfah slippers, the standard Hawaiian footwear known as flip flops to the tourists. He mumbled to himself. "If we don't finish this job I won't get money fo' buy new slippahs."

Makoa looked up to the truck. His long face grew a large smile. Pono found what he had been searching for. He tenderly carried a life-size stuffed Santa Claus, complete with a plastic flower lei. Pono handed the jolly one down to his happy friend.

"Worth the wait?"

"Santa's da' man!"

Makoa handed Santa back to Pono, who reverently carried the figure to the stage, setting it down with care. Makoa became serious and said, "I been a good boy Santa. No more lava rock this year." Pono laughed. Makoa chuckled at himself then asked,

"What do you want for Christmas?"

Pono's laugh turned to a frown. A painful, profound frown. He crawled back into the truck, pulled out a tall Christmas tree. Melancholy, he handed one end down to Makoa, clambered out with the other end, and headed towards the stage.

Both were silent.

Something was definitely wrong. Pono was the happiest person that anybody knew. Always quick with a joke, and ready to smile at anything. No matter what happened, Pono could find the humor in it.

But not today.

They righted the tree and steadied it. Makoa looked at his somber friend and put a hand on his shoulder. "Brah, what's going on?"

Pono bit his lip and turned to Makoa, holding back tears. "It's Kupa'a."

Makoa was shocked. "Problems with your wife?".

The giant Pono slumped, as if his massive strength had suddenly drained from his body.

"We haven't talked in weeks."

"Nothing?"

"You know how it goes. I said something, she said something, and now, nobody says nothing."

"What, you two just sit and stare at each other?"

"I barely see her. She leaves early, takes care of her mom all day, and doesn't come home 'til after dinner."

"She doesn't talk to you at all?"

"She goes right to bed." Pono exhaled hard. "I think she's just tired of me. And I don't blame her."

"Brah, you gotta do something to break the ice."

Pono nodded. Gloomy, the two went back about their business, then Makoa cracked a sly grin. "But you know Pono, most men would be happy with a wife that nevah talks!"

Now, Pono was the type who would usually roar at such a line, but this time, he turned to his friend and could only muster a half-hearted smile. That's when Makoa knew that this was very serious.

"What you gonna do Pono?"

"Christmas is almost here. I got to buy her a gift, something really special. Something that shows her how much I love her."

"Like what?"

"You know Kupa'a. She has simple tastes."

"Judging from who she married, she has plain bad taste!" Pono had to grin at that. He shoved his friend playfully. The two stood up and went back to work. Pono spoke, thoughtful.

"But there is one thing she has always wanted. A Hawaiian bracelet. We could never afford one, but I'm sure that would change things for us."

"Well go get her one!" Pono just stared at his friend until Makoa finally understood.

"Oh. You still can't afford it."

CHAPTER TWO

Pono and Makoa had the stage nearly finished. Santa was in place next to the tree, large ornaments, and giant presents. A band was tuning up for a sunset performance, lightly strumming some favorite local Christmas tunes that wafted from the slack key guitars on the gentle breeze.

Pono and Makoa stood back and admired their work as tourists snapped photos of the Christmas scene on a tropical beach.

From the street, a man dressed in Hawaiian business attire ambled up towards the stage. Makoa spotted him first. He nudged Pono, who was too wrapped up in enjoying the festive atmosphere. Makoa nudged him again, harder. Pono turned and saw him. A look of dread came over both their faces.

Pono addressed the man as he approached.

"Hello, Boss."

The man, quite reserved, replied. "Pono. Makoa."

Makoa broke the tension. He motioned towards the stage. "Pretty good, uh?"

"Yes, well done." He took in a deep breath, exhaled heavily. "Pono. I need to speak to you."

Pono and Makoa looked at each other. They knew what this meant. They'd both been there before. Makoa patted Pono's shoulder to give him strength.

The businessman walked away, joined by Pono. Makoa looked on from a distance as the two chatted. He could read the man's lips as he said "I'm sorry, Pono." Pono bowed his head ever so slightly, and accepted a handshake. The man shuffled away.

Pono returned to Makoa, forced a smile and said softly, "Sorry braddah, looks like you're on your own." Makoa shook his head.

"I can't believe they let you go a week before Christmas."

Pono plopped himself down next to Santa. "How am I ever going to buy Kupa'a a gift?" He slumped.

Makoa put on a positive face. "There's got to be other jobs out there."

Pono nodded, struggled to smile then said, "Well, there is one bright side."

"What's that?"

"I don't have to listen to you all day!" The two broke into laughter.

Makoa rammed his shoulder into his friend. "That's my Christmas present to you!"

Pono grew a big goofy smile. "Best gift evah!" They fell all over themselves in hysterics, forgetting reality, if just for a moment.

CHAPTER THREE

Amorose Pono dragged himself up the stairs of the run-down, cinder block apartment building he called home. Runny nosed toddlers played in the stairwell as the wail of infants echoed throughout the complex. Pono usually didn't even notice. This was his normal. But today the children made him think of his future. A future he was sure of before things went so wrong.

People would often ask if Pono and Kupa'a had any kids. Their response was always, "Not yet, but we want to someday." Pono's mind focused on the word "we." Were they still a "we?" Would their plan of being parents together become a long-lost regret? Pono loved children. Kupa'a used to say that it was because he was a big kid himself. Many times he daydreamed of watching Kupa'a snuggling their own child. Would that ever come to be? Pono choked up again. His emotions were in shambles.

He struggled to get the key in the lock, then jostled the handle up, down, back and forth until the bolt finally turned. The door creaked open and Pono stepped into the tiny living room that also housed a minuscule kitchen. The rust-pocked fridge was as old as the building and worked about as well. Pono tugged at the handle, peered inside. The contents told the story of life in the Kalele residence. Half a jumbo loaf of generic sandwich bread, a warehouse-sized container of the cheapest peanut butter, a jar of guava jelly, a jug of milk, and a big block of government cheese.

Pono especially hated the cheese. He was a proud man. With all the times that he was laid off from work, he never once went on unemployment. He didn't begrudge those that did, but it wasn't for him. The free cheese reminded him of how he yelled at Kupa'a for accepting it from a friend when times were particularly rough.

Kupa'a. Pono's heart ached at the thought that he was losing her. He wished he had never raised his voice at her. She just wanted to bring extra food in the house and, because of his pride, he got angry.

He thought of the time she spent money on a special birthday gift for him, a Hawaiian quilt with his favorite pattern, ulu, the local breadfruit. It reminded him of his childhood home of Waimanalo. He made her return it because it cost too much. There were also the times he scolded her for the way she squeezed the toothpaste tube in the middle, and countless other things.

Pono slumped. It was all so stupid, so picky. He had slowly chipped away at her for no good reason. Now, all that mattered in this world was for them to be the way they once were. So in love that nothing could disturb their peace. Not circumstances. Not work. Not poverty. Pono feared that he had come to his senses too late.

Pono plopped down on the worn couch that was striped with silver duct tape to keep it together. He pulled up a TV tray with bread, peanut butter, and jelly then looked at the clock on the stove. 5:59. He glanced over at the door, exhaled hard, pulled out two slices. Then he heard something that made him sit up straight; footsteps outside the door. Hope returned in a flash. Could she be home for dinner tonight? Could the ordeal be over? But instead of keys in the lock, there was knocking. A sharp, distinctive knocking. Pono's face filled with dread.

He slowly approached the door, preparing himself for the assault. This was going to be bad. He opened the door and there stood his worst nightmare: Aunty K. She was an 83-year-old local woman who barely made five feet tall. Her Hawaiian name was longer than she was, so everyone called her Aunty K for short. As tiny as she was, her ninety pound frame made Pono quiver with fear. She glared up into Pono's eyes and spoke with a raspy, pointed voice.

"Pono, do we have to do this again?"

"I so sorry Aunty, I'll have the money for you by the end of the month."

She just stared up at Pono, who felt lower than her thrift store loafers.

"This has gone on long enough Pono. Christmas Eve. If you aren't caught up by then, I will have no choice but to start eviction proceedings."

"But Aunty."

She cut him off. "I'll be back Christmas Eve, 6 p.m." She strode away.

Pono closed the door, nearly broken.

Later that evening, Pono straightened up the kitchen. As he turned back towards the couch he heard keys in the door. The big man froze. The door swung open, and a vision of beauty glided in like a soft Hawaiian breeze. Kupa'a was a blend of many local flavors. Hawaiian, Filipino, Chinese, and a hint of Portuguese. Beyond her striking features was her elegant poise. As Pono watched her deftly close the door with barely a sound, he thought, as he had many times before, that she must be descendant of royalty. A long-lost princess stuck in this lowly hovel that he provided. He didn't feel worthy of even being in her presence.

As Kupa'a turned toward the bedroom, their eyes met. For a brief moment, they held each other's gaze, but neither spoke. Kupa'a looked down and scurried to the bedroom, quietly closing the door behind her. Pono wanted to speak but couldn't. He was sure it was over.

CHAPTER FOUR

Pono slipped out of the house early. He didn't want Kupa'a to know that he'd lost his job, so the best thing to do was to leave at his normal time and find another one as soon as possible.

Pono walked down to the corner of Punchbowl and King Street. Honolulu Hale (Honolulu City Hall) was decorated for the season complete with a gigantic Christmas tree. But the big attraction, which showed everyone that the Christmas season had officially arrived, were the two huge, glistening statues of Santa throwing a shaka and Mrs. Clause in her muumuu. The two were happy, barefoot, and carefree, cooling their feet in the fountain. This scene usually brought great joy to Pono, but it also reminded him that the big day was fast approaching.

Questions darted through Pono's head. How was he going to pay the rent and have money to buy something so special for Kupa'a that it would break the silence? Could he find another job? Where would he find the right bracelet? And if he got a bracelet, would his plan even work? It was overwhelming.

Pono searched his crowded brain for inspiration. Suddenly, words from the chorus of a famous local song about a Hawaiian fighter rang in his brain. He remembered listening to it as a teenager, and his grandmother asking him if he knew what the Hawaiian words he was singing meant. When he said no, Grandma said solemnly, "Mai nana hope, imua. It means do not look back, go forward, with strength." Grandma went to him, put a tender hand on his shoulder, and looked into her grandson's eyes. "Pono, there will be times that life knocks you down. In those times, remember these words of your ancestors."

Pono still got chicken skin (goosebumps) all these years later just as he did when Grandma first gave him that advice. That was exactly what Pono needed. He had to summon the courage of his ancient roots and, despite the looming obstacles, go forward. Imua.

Recharged, Pono looked up at the Santa, grinned, and fired a shaka back at him. He held his head up and strode off.

But it was not easy for Pono to keep his spirits up as the day wore on. Pono started at the library across from Honolulu Hale, searching the internet for jobs. No luck. Since then, he had been walking the scorching streets for hours, searching door to door for employment. He heard the same thing over and over again: "Come back after the new year." He kept telling himself that he had to keep going.

He turned a corner and came upon a row of small mom-and-pop shops at the edge of Chinatown. An object in one of the windows caught Pono's eye. Mesmerized, he felt himself pulled towards it. He walked up to the display, his eyes wide. Hanging there was a simple but elegant gold Hawaiian bracelet. There it was. The answer to all his woes. It was absolutely perfect. Pono composed himself, and stepped inside.

A slender, modestly dressed middle-aged woman greeted him with a sincere, kindly voice. "Merry Christmas. Can I help you with something?" Timid, Pono swallowed hard, then fumbled over his words as he tried to speak. The kind woman sensed his discomfort and asked, "What is it?" Pono relaxed. "Well, I was wondering if, by any chance, you might have a job opening."

The woman's face showed true compassion as she gently denied him. "I'm so sorry. I run this little shop by myself. I can't afford to pay for help."

Pono thanked her and turned to leave. He paused on his way out and peered longingly at the bracelet. The owner noticed and went to the display.

"Are you interested in this?" Pono nodded, but then looked down. She understood immediately.

"But you need a job to pay for it." Pono said yes with his eyes.

The shopkeeper placed a comforting hand on Pono's shoulder. "She must be very special."

Pono peered up, love in his eyes. "More than you can imagine."

Pono's eyes strayed to a small sign behind the register. It read, "Payment Plans Available." Pono's heart leapt.

"Aunty, can you put me on a payment plan? I promise I will pay it back. With interest!"

The owner peered at the large man with a tender look of empathy. She spoke softly.

"What's your name?"

"Pono. Pono Kalele."

"Pono, I can see how much you want this bracelet."

Pono was hopeful. The woman continued.

"But I can't do that to you. It's clear that you really can't afford this right now. If I sell it to you, it will just make matters worse."

Pono had been so focused on securing the gift that he hadn't thought it through. But she was right. What would happen if he gave a beautiful piece of jewelry to Kupa'a, but then couldn't pay the rent and they got evicted? What would she think of him then?

A sheepish Pono said, "Thank you for looking out for me, Aunty."

She nodded. Pono chuckled.

"I guess it's not a great idea to ask for credit right after I asked for a job!"

The two laughed together.

Pono started to leave. Just before he was past the door, the woman called to him.

"Pono, I do know someone who might have something."

Pono's eyes opened wide. Her face showed concern as she continued.

"But…"

Pono pleaded. "I'll do anything."

She searched for tactful words then finally blurted out, "He's not easy to work with."

Pono's face showed that he was up for the challenge.

The woman wrote down an address on a slip of paper and handed it to Pono. "Tell him Aunty Malama sent you."

CHAPTER FIVE

Pono crept down a small, disheveled alley in Kakaako. He was amazed to think that this was merely two blocks from the stunning views of Ala Moana Beach Park. He looked up at the peeling sign on an opaque window which read, "Unko Kimo's Plate Lunch." This was the spot. Pono pushed on the faded red door.

The place smelled of stale carpet, spilled beer, and rancid cooking oil; typical of this type of dimly lit, back alley eatery. Pono walked in quietly, afraid of who or what he might see. The crashing of glass startled him, but the subsequent yelling showed Pono where to find the owner. Pono went just beside the counter and looked back into the ramshackle kitchen. He shifted his body to the side to get into the aggravated man's field of vision. The owner noticed and turned his fiery eyes from the broken glasses to the Polynesian. "We're closed."

"Sir, I'm here for the job."

"What job?"

"Aunty Malama sent me. She said you might have something." Pono motioned down towards the mess. "Do you want me to clean that up?" The man peered down at the tangle of shards, then back to Pono. His anger dissipated to mere contempt. "Go ahead."

Pono carried the jagged remnants on a piece of cardboard out into the alley. He squinted as his eyes adjusted to the bright December sun. He carefully balanced the load with one hand as he lifted the lid on a dumpster. The stench made the strong man turn away and wince with disgust. He deposited the debris and quickly backed away. He wiped his hands and rushed back in. Kimo met him there, stern.

"They're demolishing the building. Putting up another high-rise. We have to be out of here by January 1st, but if this dump isn't pristine, they'll keep my rental deposit."

That didn't make sense to Pono. "But they're tearing down the building."

"It's just business. Cold, hard business."

Pono allowed himself to hope. "I can help you clean up."

The man snarled, "I don't want your help."

Pono stepped back, surprised at the outburst and disappointed. The owner continued, his face contorting into a rage as he spit out the words.

"You will clean it up by yourself. Minimum wage, but I'll pay cash at the end of each day." Pono agreed immediately. Despite the deplorable conditions, Pono was thrilled.

CHAPTER SIX

Pono reached into the back of a high shelf in his tiny kitchen. His sore fingers, rubbed raw from pushing a rough-handled broom all day, grasped a jar. It was half-full of cash, both bills and coins. He twisted the top off, emptied the contents onto the counter, and pulled a wad of bills out of his pocket to add to the pile. He started counting.

As he finished, he did a quick mental calculation, then sighed and shook his head. He wasn't going to earn enough to make the rent by the time Aunty K returned. What to do? Pono could only think of one thing: pawn shop. That was the answer. But what did he have that was worth anything? He looked around the kitchen and living room. Nothing. He went into the bedroom, opened the closet. An old basketball? Worn out clothes? Worthless. He continued to rummage. Nothing.

As he looked around the room, his eyes lighted on their old radio/CD boom box. Thanks to that machine, he and his Kupa'a shared many wonderful times together enjoying music. But that cherished habit faded away with their relationship. Pono picked it up, nostalgic. After a few moments of deliberation, he put on his warrior face. It was more important to pay the rent than to keep a worn out remnant of another time. He left with the radio under his arm.

The only thing more sketchy than the pawn shop was the owner. The hunched over, weasel of a man stared at the boom box, then up at Pono, incredulous. "Are you kidding me?"

Pono did his best impression of a salesman. "It has a great sound."

"It belongs in a museum. This is the age of iPods and tablets. Nobody wants this thing."

"Can't you make an offer?"

The owner lifted the boom box and looked it over one more time before unceremoniously plopping it down on the counter. "Five bucks."

"That's it?"

The owner just stared, silent. His eyes locked on his victim and he didn't move a muscle. The shrew made a fine living off of the despair of others because he was a master of negotiation. He knew this silent treatment would eventually make the inexperienced big man sweat. Pono did start to feel uncomfortable under the crafty negotiator's gaze and glanced away. He began to think that five dollars was better than nothing. As the pressure mounted, Pono was about to agree. That was before he looked up and read the owner's face. It had taken on a devilish look. He actually enjoyed putting Pono in such a heartbreaking dilemma. He exuded a wicked sense of superiority that came from holding a desperate man's fate in his hands, and being able to take advantage of his need. It was a game that he reveled in. But Pono was not going to give him the satisfaction. He felt a flash of heat in his veins. Pono straightened up tall and scooped up the radio like saving a baby from a jackal. "No thanks."

The vermin's eyes twitched. "Okay, I'll give you seven."

Pono glared at the repulsive creature, who shrunk back under the gaze of the proud Hawaiian. Pono turned and marched out.

Pono hadn't felt that kind of fire since he was a much younger man. Maybe he wouldn't make the rent. Maybe he would have to tell Kupa'a that they were going to be evicted, which would surely be the breaking point. But at least he still had his pride. Pono quickly realized that while pride is good, it wasn't what he was after. What he really wanted was Kupa'a.

Pono worked hard. Very hard. It was dirty, backbreaking, menial labor, but he did his best every day. He kept his spirits up, always giving a smile to his gloomy boss.

Pono finished up another work day. Although tired and sweaty, he gratefully accepted the cash that the boss paid him. Today, Pono hesitated before he left. He finally spoke in a voice just above a whisper. "Boss. Do you need me tomorrow?"

At first the boss didn't understand the question. Then it dawned on him. "Oh, Christmas." The boss shook his head. "No, take the day off."

Pono wished him a merry Christmas and rushed out.

CHAPTER SEVEN

Pono squirmed on his old couch in anticipation. The jar of cash, now nearly full, sat on his dinner tray but his eyes were on the clock. It changed to 6:00. He turned and stared expectantly at the opening below the bottom of the door. He heard the footsteps, saw the moving shadows, then the knocking. Pono rose slowly, morose. He dreaded what was coming.

Small, wrinkled, spindly fingers counted out the money. The bills were stacked and Aunty K was now making piles of quarters. Pono sat next to his landlady on the couch, awaiting the verdict. She counted the piles of quarters. "947, 948, 949, 950." Her features grew even more tense than usual." She glared at Pono, her tone severe.

"You're fifty dollars short."

"I promise I'll have it in a few days."

Aunty K spoke with an icy tone. "But you are already over three weeks late. I was very clear with you. Today is the deadline."

Pono slumped. He knew she wouldn't budge. When she said something she meant it. No leeway, ever from Aunty K. She was always exactly on time and demanded payment to the penny. So contrary to the Hawaiian way. Pono figured that's why she always seemed uptight.

The austere woman opened her purse and reached in. Pono thought that this was typical of her too. She must have already prepared the eviction papers so she wouldn't have to make another trip. No wasting time or bus fare in her world.

The landlady withdrew her hand and produced some papers. But they weren't what Pono expected. These were small papers, green papers. Pono was confused. Aunty K reached out and gently placed two twenties and a ten on Pono's pile of cash.

Pono looked at it, astonished. He looked back to the woman. She let a kindly smile emerge, one that Pono had never before seen. She spoke with a gentle voice.

"Merry Christmas, Pono."

Pono wasn't sure what to do, so he did what came naturally. He gave her a big hug. She pushed him away.

"Eh, no get frisky with me!"

They shared a welcome laugh. She scooped all the money into her purse then rose to leave. Pono opened the door for her.

"Thank you Aunty. Thank you so much."

With a warm smile she said, "Give my best to Kupa'a." Then her stern demeanor returned. "But you get the money for this month!"

"I will Aunty." She gave him a grin and parted.

Pono stumbled back and plopped onto the couch. A Christmas miracle. He yelled out, triumphant. "Chee hoo!" Such a large load lifted off his shoulders. Then another reality hit. Christmas was tomorrow. They weren't getting evicted, but there was still no money for a present. No chance to break the cold spell. He looked at the clock. 6:20, and no Kupa'a. His stomach twisted.

Pono made his way into the bedroom and peered at the radio, now back in its normal place. This used to be such a happy place, a sanctuary of love and laughter that kept out all of their worldly worries. The big man's heart clenched. Should he give up? Accept defeat? Once again, he heard his Grandma's voice. "Imua." Pono knew that he had to go out and try for one more Christmas miracle.

Hours of searching yielded absolutely nothing. It was late when an exhausted Pono made his way back past Honolulu Hale to catch the bus home. Shaka Santa and Tutu Mele (Mrs. Claus) had attracted an especially large crowd this night before the big day. Santa and Tutu looked happier than ever under the bright lights. Pono regarded the festive scene of families strolling in the seventy five degree night air with mixed emotions. Once again, he was going home empty handed. He felt like a colossal failure. Tomorrow, a day reserved for rejoicing, would surely be the day that sealed his fate. The big man was scared.

As he crossed the street to get to the bus stop, Pono noticed a large crèche display of the Christ Child in the manger. It was in the opposite direction of the bus, but Pono felt compelled to go closer. He approached the scene slowly, with reverence. Each character was in their proper place. Joseph, Mary, the wise men, a few animals, and the Baby Jesus. Pono then noticed another figure, one not always included in nativity scenes. It was a sincere child standing next to the manger with his drum at the ready. It was the little drummer boy, and the Baby Jesus was smiling gratefully at him.

Pono was surprised at how touched he felt. When Pono was a boy, he loved to hear this story, but tonight it held much greater significance for him. Pono regarded the drummer boy and said softly, "I have no gift to bring." Instead of sadness, a humble, kindly smile came to the big man's face. He leaned in toward the drummer boy and said, "Braddah, you and me are in the same canoe!" He allowed himself a chuckle, but the levity just lasted a moment. Pono became somber. "Except I don't even have music. I've got nothing."

CHAPTER EIGHT

It was early Christmas morning, but Pono hadn't been able to sleep at all. He lay there on the couch, his forlorn eyes staring at the clock. As the glowing digits changed to 5:30, Pono reluctantly pulled himself up. He sat there pondering, searching for direction. He set his eyes on the kitchen drawer. He inhaled deeply, then blew it out. He pulled his large frame up, tiptoed into the kitchen and quietly opened the drawer. He pulled out a sewing kit along with a half spool of white thread. Bleary eyed, he stole out of the apartment.

Minutes later, as the early morning rays peaked over the Koolaus onto Honolulu, Pono sat alone under a blooming plumeria tree. Although the enchanting fragrance of the yellow blossoms enveloped him, large, salty tears rolled down the big man's face. Needle and thread in hand, Pono prepared the only gift he could afford. He was making a flower lei for his dear wife Kupa'a. One flower after another, he lovingly strung the lei with all the aloha he had.

Pono paused just outside of his apartment and took a deep breath before gently opening the door. Christmas music wafted into the living room from the bedroom and Pono saw Kupa'a, her back to him, humming to a soulful local version of "O Holy Night" as she rearranged a small porcelain crèche on the counter. Kupa'a heard the door close. She paused for a moment, then slowly turned to face her husband.

Pono, holding the lei behind his back, stood there, frozen. They both regarded each, silent, tentative. After a few exceedingly long moments, Pono forced his shaky legs to carry him up to his wife. He looked her in the eyes, then peered down and away, ashamed.

"I'm sorry Kupa'a. This is the only gift that I could get for you."

He took his hands from behind his back, lifted the fragrant lei and gently placed it over Kupa'a's head. He softly kissed her on the cheek, then stepped back. What followed were more agonizing moments of silence. Pono wondered if it would ever end. Finally, Kupa'a spoke. Her voice was velvety, but her tone was solemn.

"I guess you're wondering why I've been coming home late."

Pono nodded yes.

Kupa'a said, "Wait here."

Pono's eyes followed her as she glided into the bedroom. Pono was not sure what to think. He heard her shut off the Christmas music. Pono slumped. That was surely a bad sign. The following moments of silence seemed interminable. But what happened next left Pono puzzled.

He saw Kupa'a's hand reach outside the bedroom door and place the old boom box on the floor. There was some rustling from within the room, then her hand reappeared and she pressed the play button. A lovely traditional instrumental Hawaiian Christmas song began to play.

And then, it happened.

Kupa'a emerged from the room resplendent in her sole traditional Hawaiian dress, the one that she wore when they were married. Her face was serene and lovely, and her neck was adorned with the flower lei that Pono made for her. Kupa'a's eyes locked with Pono's, and after a few still moments, she began to move. Her knees bent, her hips began to sway, and she moved her hands with an astounding grace. Kupa'a was performing a heartfelt, loving hula for the man she loved. And it was breathtaking.

Pono was overcome with emotion. He rushed to her. Husband and wife embraced and swayed together to the music as one. The music, the dance, the scent of the flower lei, and their tears of joy washed away all the hurts of the past. In this moment, on this Christmas Day, the two shared the greatest gift of all; their love for each other.

EPILOGUE

Years went by and the couple grew happier than ever before. Pono's boss opened a new café and hired Pono to be his ambassador of aloha. Pono relished the job of greeting customers and making them feel welcome, and his kindly spirit even rubbed off on his boss. The business became very successful, and Pono's family shared in that success. He even got Makoa a stable, full time job at the café, and the two continued their teasing ways throughout their workdays.

And yes, Pono and Kupa'a had two beautiful children. Aunty K never had to visit again to get back rent, but she did arrive every Christmas Eve to go with the Kalele family on their annual visit to see Santa and Tutu Mele at Honolulu Hale. They would make the rounds, then go across the street to the crèche where the proud parents would tell the kids about the Christmas long ago when all they could afford was a handmade lei and a hula dance. And it was still their favorite Christmas of all. It was their Aloha Christmas.

www.ingramcontent.com/pod-product-compliance
Lightning Source LLC
Chambersburg PA
CBHW040437150626
46551CB00023B/88